Nigh

book 1

Written by

Marie Bilodeau

Nigh - Book 1 Copyright © Marie Bilodeau 2015

Cover and Interior Illustrations Copyright © 2015
by Kerri Elizabeth Gerow. All rights reserved.

Cover Design by Designs by Lynsey
http://www.designsbylynsey.co.uk/

Editing by Gabrielle Harbowy
http://gabrielle-edits.com/

Copyediting by Jessica Torrance

All rights reserved. Reproduction or utilization of this work in any form, by any means now known or hereinafter invented, including, but not limited to, xerography, photocopying and recording, and in any known storage and retrieval system, is forbidden without permission.

First edition

ISBN
978-0-9940439-1-7

This is a work of fiction. Names, characters, places and incidents are the products of the author's imagination or are used fictitiously and are not to be construed as real. Any resemblance to actual events, locales, organizations, or persons, living or dead, is entirely coincidental.

S&G Publishing
PO Box 30063
Greenbank North PO
Ottawa, ON
CANADA K2H 1A3

To *Katherine Gallant* of the Graham Clan,
for being so freaking awesome.

(You'd also kick faerie ass. I want you on my
Faerie Apocalypse Survival Team.)

Acknowledgments

Nigh was a labour of much love, and many people contributed, whether they realized it or not. I first got the idea for Nigh at a storytelling show, where I had a vision of a show that would be supported by a book, and vice versa. So, first and foremost, thanks to the Ottawa Storytellers for their love of stories and fostering of the community.

Adam Shaftoe, from The Page of Reviews, who seeded the idea for a novel serialization (this is on you!).

My family, as always, is a source of inspiration: Kerri Elizabeth Gerow, Jessica Torrance, Jean-François Bilodeau, George and Ada, Suzanne Desjardins, Gilles Bilodeau and Nicole Caouette, Katherine and Martin Gallant, Karen and Dave Henderson, Xander and Isabelle.

To the Gerow/Taverner family for sharing stories, names, a hometown and some fun facts.

Thanks to Kathryn Hunt for sharing faerie knowledge and to Darrell Kouri, for sharing his knowledge and expertise of cars. And to Derek Künsken, Linda Poitevin, Karen Dudley and Nicole Lavigne for constant cheerleading.

They say the end is nigh, dear friend,
The world has passed its prime,
And we must bid good bye, dear friend,
To all the happier time.

- The Heart's Tragedy in Fairyland -
- Arthur Edward Waite -

Nigh

book 1

Written by

Marie Bilodeau

Chapter 1

THE SMALL gear popped out and tumbled to the floor, the desk lamp lighting its fall before it vanished into the darkness below the workbench.

"Damn it!" Alva flicked back a sweat-dipped strand of rust-coloured hair that escaped her braid, and crouched to find the escapee. She felt under the workbench with oil stained fingers, but calluses blocked any sensation resembling a small gear.

"Argh, under-the-workbench gross." She stood back up, disgusted, wiping her hand on the leg of her jeans.

"What's that? You're gonna clean under the workbench?" Gruff's voice boomed behind her.

"Oh ya," she turned, eyebrow raised. "Next thing you'll tell me, you expect me to mop the floors, too!"

"Clean shop is a busy shop, Al."

She grinned. "It IS clean. Cleanest in town! As long as you don't look under the workbenches." She sat on the stool, the innards of the watch laid bare before her. Intricate little swirls hugged gears and tumbled into small notches, so many that Alva didn't know where to start. Each tiny gear did so much, an intricate system of metal and planning that turned time itself.

She sighed and gently closed the watch. Gruff's dirty overalls blocked her peripheral vision. "I thought you were gonna save your money to get that fixed, Al." His voice was uncharacteristically soft.

"I need to save money for Pete's school. Besides, this isn't gram's watch." She showed him the scratched, tarnished cover. She'd kept her great gram's watch in perfect condition, just like her dad had before her.

She shrugged. "I didn't want to practice on the original, but I thought that if I could practice on another watch, then maybe... I don't know. I don't think my hands are young or nimble enough anymore."

Gruff guffawed, throwing his head back, his rebellious white hair swaying with his amusement. "If your hands can't handle the small stuff, we're all in trouble!" He held up his large hand, the right thumb tweaked to the side – it had never healed right after a car had slipped off its jack and snapped it.

He sobered again. "You should keep trying. Maybe you'll repair finer things than cars someday!" He turned back to finish his inventory.

"I like repairing cars!" She screamed after him, but he just waved back without answering.

The garage had already been closed for a few hours. Neither Alva nor Gruff were in any rush to get back home, him to an empty nest, her to an empty home. Pete would be back tomorrow, at least. She hoped the university visit had gone well. Her little sister wasn't one for disclosing information on the go. Probably too lost in her own thoughts to think of texting Al.

The main shop lights were off – drivers seemed drawn like moths to a flame to a lit garage. Alva relied on a small desk lamp.

"All right," she mumbled. "My dad built trains, I fix cars, and now let's go smaller and fix a watch. Let's make this happen!"

She grabbed her flashlight and crouched again. She imagined the grit under the bench would consist mostly of dirt and maybe some food. Only the small metal gear should reflect the light. Well, she hoped there weren't too many sharp and pointy things under there, anyway.

The light beamed and blinded her for a second. She placed her cheek against the cold concrete floor, following the beam. Most of it looked like small rocks, probably all the crap the city threw on the roads during ice season.

A piece reflected the light. "Gotcha," she said, reaching in to sweep forward everything in that vicinity. She reached as far as she could, practically wedging her shoulder under the bench. She extended her fingers as far as possible, but just as she lowered her hand, something sharp pricked her.

"Son of a..." she jerked back, knocking into the bench and

throwing herself back. A hammer landed near her head.

"You okay?" Gruff called from the parts room.

"Ya, I'm fine," she answered absent-mindedly as she stared at the blood bubbling on her finger. She grabbed her old stained rag and wrapped it around the wound, holding it tightly to stop the bleeding. Once the throbbing had subsided, she removed the rag to have a closer look.

On the side of her finger, a perfect little set of holes lined up in two connected semi-circles. Just like a little jaw.

"Gruff! We've got rats in here!" Gruff stormed out of the parts room, light spilling in behind him, forming a perfect halo around his body. She would have laughed if she wasn't busy getting off the floor.

"Where!" He grabbed the wrench from his belt and slapped it on his left palm.

Alva nodded toward the bench. Faster than she thought the six-foot-some, two-hundred-and-eighty-at-least sixty-something-year-old mechanic could move, he was on his knees. He grabbed her flashlight and redirected it toward the offender, moving it around under the bench before standing back up with a grunt. "Damn bugger's gone."

His eyes lowered to where she still clutched the rag on her finger, the blood barely distinguishable from the oil stains. He mumbled and moved, much more slowly, to one of the workstations, switching on another lamp and pulling out their first aid kit.

"Well, this will do," he said, grabbing a bandage and a small bottle of hydrogen peroxide. Alva knew the drill pretty well. She had apprenticed under Gruff more than seven years ago, since a high school placement. He'd been bandaging her wounds ever since.

Washing her hands carefully, she then dried them gingerly on a clean towel, tossed it in the laundry basket and turned, wounded hand towards Gruff.

Blood trickled lazily from the wound. Gruff smiled. "Been a while since we've done this. Not since you got Big Bertha, anyway." Alva grinned and looked toward her tool belt, slung on a peg on the wall. Her modified wrench, almost two feet longer than a regular one, hung from it.

She hissed when he poured the hydrogen peroxide on the wound, the blood now covered in bubbling white foam. He ripped open a small alcohol covered swatch and wrapped it around the wound before Alva could complain.

"Damn it, Gruff. You'd already used the peroxide!"

He grinned. "Can never be too careful."

She glared at him as he finished up, pulling the swab off to examine the wound. His eyebrow shot up. "I ain't never seen a bite like this. You said a rat did it?"

"I don't know. I didn't see it. But I imagine a rat did it." She gave him a crooked grin. "If not a rat, then what?"

He bandaged her finger and shook his head. "Well, rats ain't good for business, and neither are any other biting critters. We'll have to call the exterminators in for the weekend, just in case. Can't afford to close the shop for too long – don't wanna scare folk back to their swindling dealerships. Let's call it a night, Al. You close up here."

Alva knew better than to argue. Gruff was a good man, but he expected his employees, even his favourite one, to fall in line. He shambled off to the back, banging the cabinets closed and locking them. Alva turned back to her bench. Might as well put the watch away. It wasn't really worth much, with a broken face and rusted cover, which was why she'd been able to afford it to practice on. But it was priceless as a learning tool.

Something caught her eye, a dull silver glow on the ground. She leaned down and saw, near a drop of her blood, the tiny gear, in perfect view, as though it had just rolled itself out from under the bench and now waited for her.

Her key was barely in the lock when Mrs. Gallaway opened her door. Her wizened eyes peeked left and then right, sharpening their focus on Alva, her face wrinkling from every edge.

"There was someone looking for you, Alva," she whispered conspiratorially. "A handsome lad! A gentleman caller!"

Alva managed a smile for the old lady's sake. Mrs. Gallaway suffered from a nasty combination of insomnia, loneliness and chattiness. Alva was tired and doubted this "gentleman caller" was looking for more than to try and sell her a new set of kitchen knives. Not that she'd really know what to do with those.

"Thanks, Mrs. Gallaway." Alva perked up her voice and looked off with a dreamy look in her eyes. "I'll go dress in my ball gown now and wait for my prince charming!"

Mrs. Gallaway cackled and waved Alva off as she closed her door, her laughter assailed by coughs. Alva grinned and put the key in the deadbolt. She turned it, but the familiar releasing thunk didn't occur.

Could she have forgotten to set it? No, of course not. Locking the deadbolt was second nature.

She backed away, placing her keys between her fingers for a quick, easy weapon. Crude, but capable of inflicting lots of damage if necessary. She wasn't weak and knew she could put up a fight. Unless they had a gun, of course, and blew her head off before she could reach them. But in her little town, that wasn't too likely to happen.

Her feet firmly planted, she opened the door carefully. If anyone was in her apartment, they knew she was here now. Changing her tactic, she slammed the door open in case someone waited for her behind it. The door bounced off the wall and she caught it with her booted foot, quickly turning to face the kitchen. It was empty, but someone had opened all of the drawers. She thought of stepping back and calling the cops, but she was already here and if those bastards were still here, she wanted to give them a piece of her mind. And fists.

She ignored the barely used kitchen, which she kept clean and sparse. It was definitely empty. She turned back to the corridor and

faced her living room/dining room/bedroom — a rather small room for its multiple purposes.

No one was there. The lights were all switched on, casting large shadows on her scattered belongings. They'd been there in the past two hours, after the sun had set. She stepped over her stuff and reached the converted closet Pete used for her room. It was also in shambles, her books scattered. Alva picked up her sister's favourite books on legends and myths, relieved they weren't damaged, and carefully placed them back on the small wall shelf.

"Some handsome man," she mumbled. Mrs. Gallaway meant well, but she'd probably mentioned more than she should have, hoping Alva finally had a "suitor." Damn thieves, too lazy to get jobs, yet skilled enough to pick a deadbolt without having to break down the door. Not that they'd have found anything of value here, except…

Alva crossed the living room quickly to the train set lining the back wall. It was old and too broken to be of any worth to even collectors, but it had been her dad's when he was a boy, and it was the only thing they had left of him, save for the one thing she kept hidden in the small tollbooth station. She reached carefully across the dilapidated pine trees, the bear figure with the missing forepaws, and the faded crosswalk signal, and popped the top off the little tollbooth. It was meant to go with a car set and not on a train track, but her father had loved it so much that every time the train went around the tracks, it had to stop to pay the toll.

"Popular with the customers, I bet that was!" He laughed when he showed her, when it had been just the three of them in a small, but not as small, apartment. Her long, oil-stained fingers reached in and grazed cold metal. She let out a short sigh in relief.

She rolled her fingers around the metal and gently clasped the top, pulling free the old watch her father had given her, his grandmother's watch, the only item of value they had. "If we need to, we'll pawn it. It's gotta be worth something, but still, old gram would be disappointed…"

He'd shake his head and place it back after showing it to her. The only other time she'd seen it was when he looked at it, when they'd been talking about her schooling. He had wanted her to go to university. Then Pete. He'd always worked the trains, and the rails were dying out. The trains had been a good job when he was a boy, but now he was older, scraping by with odd jobs and no formal certification in a world that demanded proof of learning over proof of knowledge and experience.

He'd wanted her to go and take higher learning. "That watch might be good enough for one year, at least. Maybe even two. I can get more odd jobs, get money for the other years in the meantime."

He was already working 80-hour weeks.

Alva had signed up for her apprenticeship the following day. "Learn as you earn," the tagline was. And she had, and she'd never once regretted it.

But her dad had always been a bit disappointed. He'd wanted

her to do more than him, working with his hands on a technology that evolved too rapidly in the span of a lifetime. But she'd loved her job. And Gruff and her dad had become fast friends. Her winning argument had been Pete. With both of them saving money, they could afford to send at least the youngest Taverner to higher education.

That had been the plan, anyway.

Al had just turned nineteen when a drunk driver sideswiped her dad, and that was that. All she had left of him were this watch and the old train set.

She half fell on the futon, which was currently set up as a couch but would become her bed later. She missed him, but this watch somehow made her feel connected to him still – the sound of his voice as he'd tell old family legends late in the night, his tinkering with it trying to make it work, the way his eyes watered when he recited his favourite pieces of literature.

She held up the watch. It wasn't tarnished – she certainly didn't let it get that way. It was gold, or a metal resembling it enough. Dad had been convinced it was worth thousands. She doubted it, but had never had the heart to tell him so.

Its value was in its beauty, and in the stories it preserved. It was intricately carved. A small village on one side, a giant pine tree swooping over a small thatched house. On the other side was just one letter, which was her great grandmother's initial. A promise that never came to pass.

She heard a thunk in the kitchen. Alva's head jerked up and she jumped to her feet, threw the watch in her pocket, grabbed her keys and leapt in the hallway and then the kitchen in two bounds.

She threw one leg back behind the other and adopted a defensive posture, bringing up her "armed" hand.

There was nothing there.

She quickly crossed to the corridor. There was no one there, either. She glanced in the kitchen.

Hadn't those drawers been open a second ago?

She was too tired. Long shifts and her obsession with fixing the watch were taking a toll. Having her place broken into was a violation she just didn't need. Alva locked the deadbolt and the handle, and slid the nearly useless chain in place. At least it would warn her if the lock picker decided to come back. That, he'd have to break.

She pondered calling the cops for a second, but nothing had been stolen as far as she could tell, and she didn't have anything else of value. Or any insurance, for that matter. She might as well save herself the hassle.

She thought about warning Pete, but she didn't want to worry her younger sister. She was off in Toronto, checking out universities and the Royal Ontario Museum with others from her class. She needed to focus on her decision, and not worry about their home.

An hour's worth of work and most of the apartment was back to its usual order. They didn't have much, but the small space fared

better when everything was organized.

It was nearing midnight and Alva almost fell into bed before thinking better of it, walking to her front door, and placing a chair under the handle.

Chapter 2

SHE COULDN'T see through the thick fog, the night too dark, the air too thick. A light pierced through, highlighting layers of fog, making the world seem both endless and walled in.

The train whistled and she realized she had been running towards it, not away from it.

Adrenaline flooded her system as she threw herself sideways, nearly falling off her bed. It took her a moment to adjust to the encroaching darkness. She pulled her shirt off her clock, which was just too bright for any sane individual seeking a good night's sleep.

It was just after 3 o'clock. She had slept for barely three hours. Her alarm would be going off in two hours and it would probably take her half that long to get back to sleep, so she decided to get up.

She yawned and stretched, dressing only by the blue light of her alarm clock. She reached down where she'd thrown her coat and yanked, but something seemed to be on it. For a moment, she thought it might be her old tabby Frank, but he'd been gone for

almost a year. She jerked her hand back, the weight falling from the coat, and it easily came. Reaching behind her while looking wildly around, she turned the light on and tried to blink away the blindness as quickly as possible.

There was nothing there.

"I need more sleep," she mumbled, embarrassed even if no one had witnessed her confusion. It didn't matter. She knew about it, and that was enough.

She threw on jeans and a sweater. She'd left her overalls at the garage, and she would throw those on before her shift. She grabbed her coat and stared at it. It looked much cleaner than she remembered. Two oil stains she distinctly remembered on her sleeve were gone. Maybe the stains had been on her sweater. Damn, that garage could get cold sometimes.

"I'm off," she said more out of habit than need. She threw her keys in her coat pocket, hesitated for a second before grabbing the watch as well.

She didn't intend to leave her one precious possession in her apartment. Not until she was certain it was safe, anyway.

Alva squinted at the flickering road. Well, the road didn't flicker, but the street lamps certainly did. It was like all the lamps in town were on the fritz. The overcast night seemed intent on inducing seizures.

She turned off Main Street, by far the most direct route to work, and decided to take the smaller streets instead. At least they didn't have street lamps, and the lack of flickering would spare her head.

She slowed down, to avoid being too noisy. Her orange 1970 Mercury Cougar had been a pet project of hers with her dad, when she'd been a teenager. She loved the feel of the steering wheel in her hands and the pull it still had. Much more satisfying than modern cars. She smiled and ran her finger on the faux-wood dash.

Her dad shouldn't have been surprised that she'd become an auto mechanic. Restoring this beast with him encapsulated some of her fondest memories. She maintained it herself and it wasn't about to fail any emissions test, but it could get a bit loud, and she didn't want to start waking up children at four in the morning. In a small town like Lindsay, they'd probably all know it was her, too.

"Woa, Percival," she said absent-mindedly as she eased off the gas. Her old, venerable car had earned its name long ago. After they'd restored it and took it for a spin, a much larger car had sideswiped them, right on the passenger side, where Alva was sitting. The already old beast had taken the hit like a knight of old, her dad had said, saving Alva from injury. The car had earned its name then, and had kept it since.

Percival hadn't had to prove himself again, but Alva still felt more secure in the old metal beast than in any new car with complicated electronics that made her want to pull her own hair out every time a new manual came out. Which was all the time.

"And why can't every dealer just use the same damn systems?" She exclaimed out loud.

A shadow ran across the road. She slammed on the brakes. She couldn't tell if she'd hit it.

She unfastened her seat belt and opened the door, dreading what she might find. A cat, or a small dog maybe. It wasn't much bigger than that. It had moved too fast for a raccoon, and the air wasn't pungent from a skunk.

She reached over to her glove compartment and pulled out a flashlight.

The street was dark save for Percival's lights, and quiet, save for the rumbling of her old motor. If she had hit the animal and it had stumbled away, she'd need to hear it. She turned off the motor before stepping out, but kept her lights on. Percival's battery was good and wouldn't let her down.

Fall coated the crisp night. Alva could already smell winter on it, felt its cool tendrils pierce her light leather jacket. She ignored the chill and crouched beside her car. There wasn't anything under it. She aimed the flashlight on the road toward where the animal had run, and there was no blood or sign of something having ever even been there.

A nearby bush rustled and she aimed her flashlight at it. She thought she spotted eyes, but they flashed away as quickly as they'd appeared. She shrugged and got back in her car. Not having to tell a family she'd run over their beloved pet was definitely her preference.

A few minutes later she pulled into the shop. She parked in the back, the night still thick. The only sound that reached her ears was that of her boots on the gravel lot.

Inside the shop, however, a familiar sound greeted her. Snoring. She sighed and tried to be as quiet as possible as she turned on her bench light and pulled out the test watch. She'd mapped most of it and hoped she understood how it worked. But every gear had to be perfectly aligned or it wouldn't keep time right. She decided she'd completely take it apart and rebuild it. Only then could she be confident she wouldn't destroy her own. Just the

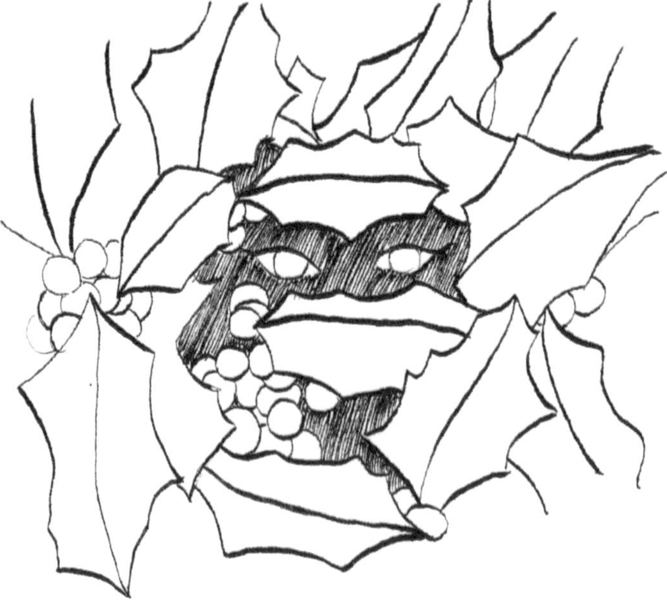

thought of the robber almost finding it last night re-motivated her to fix the watch and keep it safe.

The watch was the only thing that pointed to a past before her; her only connection to a family she never knew. And her father had always wanted to see it keep time again. In a way, it was keeping his legacy alive. Her hands would handle the same small pieces his had handled. Where Pete had inherited his love of words and literature, Al had his finesse with machines. And his love of them. This was his legacy to her, and she intended to carry it through.

Besides, she loved the challenge.

She placed every small gear and piece in a box lid, lining them up in order of removal. She was so engrossed in her work that she didn't even realize Gruff was up until the smell of coffee filled the shop. She stretched her back and groaned. It was still early, so she left everything out and went off to hunt coffee.

She headed to the back, to what could pass as a small staff kitchen. It was tiny, with a small table and two chairs squeezed onto a small fridge, coffee pot on top, but it was functional and clean. Like the rest of Gruff's shop. Gruff sat at the table, drinking coffee and reading the paper. Alva sat on the other chair, grabbing the sports section. A useless section until hockey started, but with less than two weeks to go before that happened, the trades and line-up speculations were entertaining enough.

"Up early," Gruff said, more than asked. The fridge shook as it kicked in and buzzed, making the space seem ever smaller.

"Yup. Someone broke into my place last night," she said off-handedly. Gruff lowered the paper.

"What?"

"They didn't take anything. Suppose there wasn't much to take. Well, nothing that they could have easily found, anyway."

"Al, you should have called me. I'd have helped."

Alva laughed. "With what? Clean up? They were long gone by the time I got home, Gruff."

"I would have helped with clean up. At least I'd make sure you were all right. What if the creeps came back?"

"I can take care of myself, Gruff. Aren't you the one who always tells me that I'm a woman, not a maiden, so not to get any distress ideas in mind?"

He chuckled a bit, but still looked somber when he spoke. "I know, and I know you don't need me to come protect you. But you're family, Al. Family should lean on each other during hard times."

Al nodded slowly and hesitated. Gruff spoke a good game, but he certainly hadn't leaned on her since his marriage had started unraveling. An empty nest had proved too quiet for the older couple. With the children long gone, the silence had only highlighted their lack of common interests. She'd found him sleeping in the shop quite a few times.

As if sensing her hesitation to ask him about it, Gruff folded the paper and slowly stood up. "Well, we have less than an hour before the shop opens. I'll go work on the inventory. You gonna play some more with that watch?"

"You mean study? Break apart and rebuild? Figure out all of its deeply buried secrets?"

He snorted and passed by her. "You're gonna play with the watch, then."

Alva grinned and headed to her workbench. She turned the small lamp back on and reached for her grandmother's watch in her pocket. She ran her fingers over it, wishing she could better feel the detail through the calluses on her fingers.

She looked down at the gears she'd perfectly aligned. Her eyes grew wide and she mumbled a perfect string of swears.

The thing was a mess. Parts were everywhere. Maybe the rat was back and had tried to get into her box, making a mess of the fine parts.

She took a deep breath and reined in her urge to stomp the ground in case the rat was somewhere near. The little bastard would meet its end this weekend at the hands of the exterminator. In the meantime, she had work to do. No better way to learn, she supposed. If she could figure this mess out, no watch would be a match for her from now on.

Grabbing a small gear with the bandage proved a challenge, so she pulled it off. The wound looked angry and red. It didn't hurt, at least, but the last thing she needed was some vermin infection. Gruff would send her to the emergency if she told him, so she threw some more peroxide on it and applied a new bandage. She'd go to the clinic later to if it still needed it. No point in waiting in a hospital emergency room to be stuck with a bunch of sick people.

Nothing some more peroxide and alcohol couldn't handle. She hoped.

Since she didn't dare take off the bandage again, she used the tweezers to help her move the small parts, her mouth parted in concentration. Then, as the minutes passed, her mouth was parted by hisses. And finally by swear words.

"How the bloody blazes do people work with such small parts?" She desperately wanted to turn back and fix a car, any car. She'd personally take care of a basic oil change just to deal with something she understood.

She stood up and stretched, knowing it was just fatigue and the growing throb in her finger that were making her impatient. She could figure this out – it was watch building, not rocket science.

She sighed. It was already six, and time to get started with her actual day.

She carefully closed the box and placed it in her bench. Gruff had made it clear it was hers, for her tools, some of which he'd helped her modify. There weren't many female mechanics, especially in her neck of the woods, and sometimes she just needed a longer wrench.

She yawned and headed to the kitchen to get more coffee as she planned her day. Pete was supposed to be back from her trip this

morning, so she'd need to pick her up at some point. Wouldn't serve anyone any good for Al to curl up with the rats under her workbench.

Armed with a mug of Gruff's thick as oil coffee, she headed back to her workbench, grimacing as the thick liquid coated her throat. She yawned again, surprised she wasn't about to swallow her own head, when she saw someone leaning over her bench.

It took her a moment to realize it wasn't Gruff – frame too slight, long dark trench coat, dark brown hair. It took her another moment before she found her voice.

"Hey!" She screamed, startling the man. He reacted almost immediately, grabbing her box and slipping out the propped-open door. Alva dropped the coffee, swung by the wall and grabbed Big Bertha with barely a pause, and took off after him.

"Al?" She heard Gruff shout as she leapt out of the shop. No one seemed to have crossed the road to the cemetery right in front of the shop. She ran to the right and around, but there wasn't a trace of the intruder. She slowed down and looked under the cars parked in the back. The morning was growing thick with fog, and the surrounding misty woods could hide any number of watch thieves.

"What's going on, Al?" Gruff asked, panting as he joined her. His face was completely red and Alva feared he might keel over. She clutched her wrench but tried to calm herself, for Gruff's sake.

"Some jackass in a trench coat just stole my watch!" She didn't sound nearly as calm as she'd been hoping for.

"Who the hell... ?" Gruff stormed back to the door. Alva glanced one more time at the surroundings. A few cars were lining the parking lot, and a fence to the right lead to a backyard. The woods to her left were quiet, and the whole morning smelled of burnt wood and something sweet, like baking cookies.

She turned to find Gruff. "If I find his skinny little ass, I'm breaking him in two with Big Bertha."

"I hope so. How did he get in? Did you leave the door unlocked?"

Alva was sure she'd locked it. It was such a force of habit by now. Customers loved expecting service, regardless of whether they were actually open. She certainly tried to avoid indulging them in that.

"You know I didn't."

"I know," he said simply. "Didn't you say your house was broken into last night?"

Alva hand grew numb even as she clutched Big Bertha more tightly. "Yup. By a 'gentleman caller,' or so Mrs. Gallaway called him."

Gruff walked into the shop. "I'm calling the cops. This guy is stalking you, Al. That ain't good in my books."

She sighed and followed him in. "That ain't good in anyone's book, Gruff. But what are the cops going to do?"

"I don't know, but we'll let them tell us, how's that?" He walked to the phone, leaving no room for debate.

"How about after work, Gruff?" Alva tried her luck. "We have a full slate this morning. And besides, Pete's back today. I'll have to pick her up. Can't exactly tell her I'm busy with the cops."

He looked frustrated and placed the phone back down. "All right, fine. I guess I can keep an eye on you here, anyway. But I'm walking you to the cops myself after work, and I'm going with you to pick up Pete. No arguing! Understood? "

Al nodded, knowing the look in Gruff's eyes well enough to know that was as much leeway as she was getting. The whole thing just sounded like stupid hassle. The thief probably had what he'd wanted, so he wouldn't even bother her anymore.

"Good," Gruff nodded, acknowledging her own nod. "You get the shop going – almost time to open."

Al turned to clean the rest of her workbench. Her hands were shaking a bit still from anger. She wished she could go and punch something, preferably that jackass' face.

Molly came running in, juggling her purse, lunch bag and a gym bag, even though she never went to the gym as far as Al knew. Molly shot her a grin as she tripped on her own dangling scarf and dropped everything. At least she managed to catch herself on the front desk.

"It's going to be an awesome day," she said, picking up her stuff and throwing it behind the desk. "You okay?" Molly asked when she looked at Al's stern face. Molly couldn't be much more different than Al, but they'd found a comfortable friendship in their differences. Molly had been a blessing with Pete, too, her bright personality helping to bridge the gap between the two sisters.

"Some idiot just broke in and stole that watch I was ripping up," Al said. Molly knew everything about the watch. Heck, Molly pretty much knew everything about Al.

Molly's green eyes grew wider than usual. "Oh no! Did you get him? Did you call the cops? The Avengers? Shit, did you introduce him to Big Bertha?"

Al couldn't help but laugh. Molly could work her down in two seconds flat. "Thor was busy, but Iron Man might show up later."

Molly nodded, her shoulder length tousled blonde hair bouncing up and down. "And there's no blood on Big Bertha, so I'm assuming we're not digging a hole out back just yet. Let me know when, though. I'm awesome with a shovel."

"Let's hope we get that chance soon," Al mumbled. The rest of the crew came from the back rooms, exchanging greetings and yawns.

"It's gonna be busy today," Steve, the floor manager, said. "Everyone just remembered that fall is followed by winter, and maybe winter tires are a good idea." He winked at Al and Molly. He was forty-something, kept his hair just a bit long to annoy Gruff, and had an easy laugh. Jack, Carl and Louise were setting up their tools, and it looked like everyone was ready to go.

"Showtime," Al said. Molly gave her a thumbs up as she booted the computer. She turned on the light, both garage doors rolled up and the first customers rolled in.

The phone began ringing almost immediately, Molly perching it on her shoulder as she helped a customer at the desk at the same time. The second line lit up and the third.

"We've got three calls for towings already," Molly called from the desk, the phone still in her hands, all three lines lit up like a disco ball. "And I'm guessing everyone on hold is asking for the same. Fog and black ice. A mechanic's magic payday."

Al grinned at Molly, but her friend was already back on the line. She was taking down another address when the line went dead.

"Shit. That was another one. The phones are down!"

"Someone might have hit a pole," Steve said as he walked up to Gruff. "I need all hands on deck. We're getting slammed."

Gruff nodded. "You handle the team here, I'll take Al and we'll fix as many cars as we can find. We'll bring Percival and Molly with us. Redirect the lines to Molly's cell when they're back up. She can handle it from there while making sure we get paid for outside work."

"Sounds good," Steve said, already walking away and grabbing clipboards.

"Internet is down too," Molly called out from the desk. "This is going to be a super awesome day. I told you."

"Grab your coat, Molly. And whatever we need to take payments on the go. Al, get Percival and let's head off."

Gruff headed to the back to grab his own coat. Molly grinned at Al. "Road trip!" She threw on her coat and grabbed a handful of slips for credit card payments.

Al looked outside. The mists were getting much thicker. Not rare for this time of year, but rare for this part of town. The cemetery facing the shop was almost completely covered, only a few tombstones and angels glancing through the shifting mists. Al stared for a moment, imagining every shadow as the watch thief. She grabbed Big Bertha and her tool belt.

If the day was kind enough, it would give her the chance to smack him good.

The mist licked Percival's chassis, long tendrils wrapping around the engine and uncoiling away to be immediately replaced by others. The fog lights barely cut the dense mass. Al concentrated on following Gruff, his tail lights frequently swept away by the mists. She gripped the steering wheel tightly. The radio was off so all her senses could focus on the road and not smashing into anything. Or anyone.

Molly sat quietly beside her. Even the chatty woman was silenced by the tension. She pulled her coat more tightly and Al realized she was also getting chilly. The day was cooling down quickly. She turned the heat on and, in the second it took to reach the controls, almost slammed right into Gruff. She slammed on the brakes instead and skidded to a stop. The tow truck resumed slowly. Al barely saw the traffic light overhead that had prompted the stop. Good thing Gruff had spotted it. Then again, when you're the only one spotting something, chances of being smacked into are still fairly high.

"This is fun," Molly mumbled from the passenger seat.

Al grinned. "Well, now we know why so many cars need help this morning!"

"Smackdown on the roadside," Molly said, though her usual laughter was strained.

Al tried to think of something light to say but came up blank, too focused on tracking Gruff and keeping a healthy distance from him at the same time.

"We should be almost at the first site," Al said. She couldn't see the road signs very clearly, but hers was a small town and she knew the layout by heart.

"Great. Now I can..." Molly never finished. The tow truck in front of them suddenly spun sideways and around, the sounds of shattering windows and bent metal echoing across the street. Al had barely registered the smash before she stopped Percival and leapt out.

Molly scrambled behind her.

"Careful, there might be another car!" Al cried out as she reached the cabin of the tow truck. Its passenger side was badly dented, and Gruff looked about as dented. The airbags hadn't deployed from the side collision, and the left side of his face was covered in blood.

"Gruff, are you okay?" Al asked as she threw the door open.

"I'm fine," Gruff insisted, waving her away.

"Gruff, stop being a stubborn ass and let me look you over. How do you feel?"

"Fine. Bit of a headache, but nothing bad."

"If that was me there, you'd be calling an ambulance."

He gave her a slight grin. "Boss' choice. Go check on the other driver. I'm probably bigger than them, and they probably took this head on."

Al nodded and jumped off the truck. "Molly, can you stay with him?" Molly nodded, looking determined. Al was grateful for Gruff's insistence that all of his staff have first aid training.

Molly leaned in to chat with Gruff, to keep him talking and awake as she checked his head and neck.

Al peered through the mist but couldn't see another car. She walked toward the curb, where the collision's trajectory might have sent it, but nothing was there. It wasn't likely that it would have gone anywhere. Looked like it had t-boned the tow truck, so that should have stopped it in its tracks.

She skirted along the back of the truck. Its right side panel was dented in, but at first glance it seemed repairable. They wouldn't be towing anyone back to the shop today. The pavement beside the truck was the bigger mystery. It was dented in and broken, like something heavy had smashed it. Or a sink hole, maybe? Still, it wouldn't have damaged the truck like that.

Al finished her 360 of the truck and joined Molly and Gruff. Gruff was still sitting and Molly had him going on about old cars. He stopped when he spotted Al.

"Is the other driver okay?" He asked, concerned.

Al shook her head. "I honestly don't know. I couldn't find the other car."

"That car hit hard. I doubt they got far."

"Couldn't see a thing, Gruff. And couldn't even tell what type of car it was. A freaking tank, because they didn't leave behind any of their chassis when they smashed the truck!"

"Or a good old car with armour like iron," Molly mumbled, pulling her coat tighter. It was getting chillier. Their breath added to the mist and condensation formed on every surface, including themselves.

"Didn't even see them coming," Gruff said as Al and Molly helped him out. "Just hit me out of nowhere."

"Well, the mist isn't helping anything. Let's get you to the clinic for a checkup and head back to the shop. We'll have to make do and help the cars that make it in. Can't risk moving the truck now – who knows what damage was done."

"Ah, old reliable here would still get us home." Gruff said, still uneasy on his feet but trying to hide it. Al grabbed his arm to help support him and he didn't protest. That worried her.

They reached Percival and she was helping Gruff into the passenger seat when the first scream sounded. It echoed down the street, as though born from the fog itself.

"What the..." Molly started saying before a second scream shattered the night, from the left. And another, from the right. A car alarm sounded. And another. A shop alarm went off.

Alva looked around frantically, not able to figure out what was happening, the fog blocking all sight but also distorting sounds and spreading them around like a coat of warm wax.

"Al, get in the car," Gruff said calmly. She nodded and moved around to the driver's seat. Molly didn't need any prodding, already having scooted in the back seat.

Al slammed the door shut and turned the motor on.

"What's happening?" Al asked as she backed away from the

truck. She hit something and slammed on the brakes. She went to open the door to check what she'd hit when the back of the car was pushed up. Someone started banging on the trunk. Al couldn't see anything through her mirror, but the car kept jumping up, landing heavily on its wheels.

"Go, Al, Go!" Molly screamed from the back. Al stomped on the gas and skidded the tires, narrowly avoiding the back end of the pick-up truck as she raced down Main Street.

"Slow down, Al. Visibility ain't good," Gruff gently reproached from the passenger seat.

"What the hell was that?" Molly screamed from the back. Gruff reached around and put a big hand on her shoulder. She calmed down immediately, but Al could see her big eyes in the rearview mirror. It would have been funny if she hadn't been terrified.

"Let's get you to the hospital," Al said as she slowed down a bit.

"No," Gruff argued. "Back to the shop. Gotta check on the guys and find out what's going on."

"Are you kidding? You took a bad hit, Gruff. We're getting you to the hospital." Al glared at him. "Say no again and I'll add to your injuries."

Gruff looked at her darkly. "The shop is on the way to the hospital," Molly piped up from the back. "How about we swing by there first and then head to the hospital? Let's at least make sure everyone knows we're not answering any more calls."

Al and Gruff both nodded. At least it was still early morning and every shop was still closed. Distant car alarms still pounded the mists.

She was just about to turn off Main Street when glass rained down on them. Al hit the brakes. Shop alarms went off all around them. Through the fog, Al could see a couple of shops, their windows shattered. She activated her windshield wipers to clear away the glass and pressed on the gas, praying her tires wouldn't be pierced by the carpet of glass crunching under them.

"Maybe go a bit faster now," Gruff said softly beside her.

She nodded and pressed down on the gas. If her tires burst, they'd still get her to the shop and she could swap them out there.

If they made it to the shop.

Chapter 3

A SIREN screeched not far away, muted by the fog.

Alva drove as fast as she dared. Her motor was loud, so pedestrians would hear her. Not that anyone was out. She thought she heard a scream. She glanced sideways at Gruff, who was pale in the seat beside her.

The fog shifted to her left, a large shadow blocking what little light was breaking through. Even over Percival's engine, she heard a loud thump and felt the ground shake. She slowed down, looking to the left at the large moving shadow.

"What the..." she began to say, but before she could finish, Gruff shouted.

"Look out!"

She swerved and narrowly avoided someone who ran screaming past. The fog swallowed him.

"I should check on him," Alva said, but Gruff put his big hand on hers to stop her from putting the car in park.

"Just keep going, Al. Let's get to the shop." Al nodded, the movement feeling slow and clunky. Her mind was trying to process everything that was happening around her, but it seemed to leave her with some detachment from reality. She forced herself to focus on driving. The shop wasn't far. Just a couple of blocks away.

Parked and crashed cars lined the side of the road. Something ran by in the fog, followed by a scream. Alva looked in the rearview mirror. She saw something large pass right behind them, silent, huge, dark. She pressed harder on the gas, but she only dared go so fast. She was glad for that as she skirted an abandoned car. Squeezing beside it proved a challenge that cost her paint on the right side of her car.

"Don't worry Al. We'll get Percival a new paint job."

"I ain't worried about that, Gruff. What's going on?" Her voice was barely a whisper above Percival's engine. She feared speaking too loudly would draw even more attention to them.

"Al," Molly said from the back. "I can't get through to anyone. The phone lines aren't playing along."

"We'll be safe at the shop," Gruff said with enough power that Al allowed herself to believe him. For now.

Al glanced back. Molly was alternating from looking puzzled at her phone to staring up, her already big eyes now impossibly large.

The mists licked Percival's hood and caressed the windshield. Al felt like she was driving through a deranged car wash, everything seeming so close and intent on coating her car.

The shop was coming up on the left. The cemetery loomed on the right, the breaking mist now surrounding the tombstones, as though dancing with the dead. A shiver ran up Al's spine.

"Al?" Molly said in a strangled voice.

Al glanced at her in the rearview mirror and then followed Molly's gaze toward the cemetery. She didn't notice anything at first, but then saw that the tombstones seemed to be moving. Nothing overt, but a tall obelisk shifted to the left. A smaller tombstone fell forward until it was at a forty-five degree angle, as though greeting the body it covered below.

"Is the ground shifting?" Al asked, Percival practically stopped now as she looked more closely. That might explain the damage to the road, but certainly not to the tow truck.

"I don't think the angel would do that just for shifting ground," Molly said, pointing to an angel statue. Al knew it well – it looked up to the sky, arms stretched out, wings spread out, as though greeting the light of day, even though trees had long ago ensured only shadow would reach it.

The angel's wings shifted and cracked down, its arms curled in and its head lowered.

"Al, get us to the shop," Gruff said calmly but sternly. "Now."

Al stopped staring at the statue, closed her mouth and loosened her grip on the steering wheel so that she could turn it. The shop looked quiet from the outside. No lights were on. The mists licked the great bay doors and infiltrated them. The doors were open, blocked by a car that had been driven halfway in and then abandoned.

The lights flickered on and then off again. Al spotted an oil spill leaking out of the shop. At least she hoped it was an oil spill.

Not one of them made a move to get out. Gruff breathed hard beside her. She glanced at him. Sweat beaded on his brow and he was pale. He needed some attention for his wounds. She needed to get him to the hospital, but he would never leave without making sure every technician and apprentice was okay.

She let go of the steering wheel and turned Percival off.

"Molly, I'm going to go in and check it out. You stay here with Gruff. If you need to, the keys are in the ignition."

She turned around to make sure Molly had heard her. Her best friend's usually warm features were set in grim determination. She nodded and squeezed Al's shoulder.

"Don't worry about us. We'll be fine. Make sure you take care of yourself, okay?"

Al managed to give her a grin. "I always do!"

Molly nodded again and put her hands around Gruff, to either comfort him or make sure he stayed there. Al wasn't sure, but was grateful either way.

"Make it fast, Al. Get them out and get yourself out."

"I will. Promise." Al took a deep breath and stepped out, gently closing the door behind her. It still seemed to echo in the quiet mist. She couldn't hear a sound. Either the entire town had gone quiet, or the mists were somehow absorbing the sound. No emergency vehicles sounded in the distance, despite the multiple accidents they'd witnessed.

Al took a step toward the shop, thought better of it and decided to head to the trunk first. She popped it open and grabbed Big Bertha. The cool metal of the wrench made her feel better, or at least more grounded. Like it was the one real thing she could count on in these surreal surroundings.

Her breath curled in front of her and she pulled her leather jacket closer around her. The day was growing unseasonably cold. The mist formed in tiny crystals, wisps she could actually see shifting in the air around her, not a blanket as usual but like tendrils.

Alva walked carefully around one. From up close, it shimmered like tiny snowflakes on a fresh bed of sunlit snow. Except the shimmer moved together, curling on itself and around objects. She forced herself to stop staring and avoided them.

She headed to the shop bay door, stepping over the liquid on the floor. It was dark, the sun blocked by the mists. Al debated whether or not to try to turn the shop lights on, but wasn't keen on attracting more attention. She headed to her bench and grabbed her big flashlight. She clutched Big Bertha more tightly.

"Steve?" She called out softly.

No answer.

"Louise? Jack? Carl?" Her voice sounded small and afraid in her own ears. She shined her light to her left, to see the rest of the shop. A car was half jacked up, the front end fallen straight off. Al forgot her worries as she rushed over. Who the hell would put a car poorly on the jacks? That was Mechanics 101 – you didn't mess around with safety.

She headed to the front and shined her light down. Carl was pinned down, his torso crushed by the large car. "Shit. Carl." She knelt by him, but his eyes were staring up and the blood around his mouth was already hard.

"Steve!" She shouted this time, in her frenzy. Why hadn't they helped him? He was just an apprentice. They shouldn't have even left him alone to jack the car!

"Louise, Jack!" She looked back down at Carl but had to look away, his open eyes filled with the same mist as outside. She stood up, swayed, steadied herself. She fought through her nausea to find the others.

Maybe she could still help them. A noise in the break room caught her attention. She slowly walked toward it, forcing herself to keep her light ahead of her and not glance back at Carl. She didn't want to look at him ever again, if she could avoid it.

The break room door was closed. Al tried to open it, but it was locked.

"It's Al. Open up!" She heard a muffled sound, maybe crying. "I've got Gruff and Molly. The car's up front and we're gonna get out of here," she said in her most reassuring voice, again forcing herself not to look at Carl. "But I need you to come on out." She

paused, then added more urgently. "We need to go."

The noise came again, this time as a more strangled cry. She thought she recognized Jack. "Jack? Jack. I'm coming in!" Al shouldered the thin door and it easily cracked and buckled, swinging in. Al practically landed on her face. She hadn't expected it to give in so easily.

Jack was curled up in the back, behind the table and by the fridge.

"Jack, we have to go," she repeated. He made another strangled cry, like a gurgling.

She took a step toward him. "Jack?"

His head was lowered on his knees. She repeated his name and he gurgled again but looked up. His eyes were white, and something was coming out of his mouth, like thousands of ants.

Al screamed and almost dropped the flashlight as she pushed herself back. She smacked into something and turned around. The thief from earlier was there, his eyes wide, looking from Jack to her. He grabbed her shoulders as though to snap her out of it.

"We have to go, now!" Al brought up her knee and connected with his groin. He folded in two and she brought up Big Bertha, connecting with his skull. He crumpled and she jumped over him, away from Jack. She skirted around Carl and ran madly, away from Jack. She almost dashed out of the shop, but turned back to grab first aid supplies for Gruff.

Something grabbed hold of her foot from under the sink. She screamed again and dropped Big Bertha as she fell back. The thief was beside her, bleeding from a cut on his scalp. He grabbed her wrench and hit whatever held her leg still, hidden in shadows.

"Come on!" He shouted, pulling her back up. She didn't hit him this time and followed him out of the shop and into Percival. She pushed him into the back, threw the first aid supplies after him, slammed her seat back and flung herself in it. He landed hard in the back beside Molly.

"Al, what…" Gruff started saying, but the thief cut him off.

"Go! Go! Go!"

The mists around them uncoiled and lashed out at Percival, taking out a side mirror. Molly screamed. Al turned the car on and punched it in reverse, gears grinding and tires screeching as she

threw it back into first gear and gunned it down the road.

To her right, the angel statue was now on its knees, its stone eyes watching them as the great branches of the cemetery came ever lower over the road, ever closer to touching the top of Percival's hood.

Al stepped on the gas and clutched the steering wheel for dear life, mists be damned.

No one told her to slow down.

Chapter 4

SHE GUNNED it down the road. An overturned truck blocked the way south so she headed north, not really thinking of destination, just trying to get away, her eyes peeled on the mists.

Sometimes she thought she saw a shape, an interruption in the roll of it. Once, a beam of sunlight hit the side of the car. But the pavement caught fire, and she fought not to close her eyes, fought to keep her hands on the wheel and Percival moving forward, her speed wavering as her uncertainty and fear paralyzed her limbs.

She took deep breaths and let them wash over her. Gruff was pale beside her, Molly reaching around the seat to comfort him.

"We need to pull over to patch you up, Gruff," Alva said, turning the wheel as much as she dared to hug the curb, and stopped.

The world outside was eerily quiet, holding its breath for what would happen next. Or having taken its final one.

Al pushed the thought from her mind and turned to the thief.

"While we patch him up, maybe you can tell us a bit about why

I shouldn't beat you to a pulp with Big Bertha?"

His eyes grew wide again, his mouth thin. To Molly's credit, she grabbed the wrench and held it before her threateningly. The thief leaned back in his seat, looking dejected.

"My name is Hector. Hector Henry Featherson." He said. He glanced up at Al through the rearview mirror but quickly glanced away to look outside. "I was trapped, and just got free. I thought I could stop it. I thought that if I got the watch in time..." He leaned his forehead against the window, closing his eyes and fogging up the glass.

Al focused on Gruff's shoulder, pulling out a sling from the first aid kit and wrapping his arm, securing it. Gruff's eyes were closed, his breathing shallow and his skin clammy.

"You holding up okay, Gruff?" she asked.

"Never been better," he whispered. She gave him some painkillers and offered him her bottle of water. He took them and leaned back against the seat.

"So," Gruff said, his voice gaining some strength already. "What's this about trying to stop this?"

Al turned around. Hector caught her eye and she thought she saw him flush before he looked away again. He reminded her of a skittish animal. She exchanged a glance with Molly, who still held Big Bertha like it was the last water on earth. Her best friend merely shrugged.

"It's, ah, it sounds crazy." His voice was soft. He ran a hand in his semi-long brown hair. Not bad looking, but she'd be more than happy to beat the pretty out of him to get some answers.

"You know what sounds crazy?" Molly piped up. "Sunbeams that set fires. Tombstones that move. Mists that seem to act with a purpose. That sounds crazy. Now dish up your crazy so we can add it to the menu, or I'll just save your face for dessert."

Al fought against a grin. Hector looked at Molly and sighed. "Not the most ladylike, are you?" he mumbled.

"You think she's not ladylike," Al said, "you should see me. Once she's through with you, I'll finish you off. Start with my stuff, thief. What were you looking to get? I assume you're the one who broke into my apartment?"

He looked embarrassed. "Yes. I had to, to try and stop this. To find the watch."

"The watch I bought? You stole it all right. I've got half a mind to…"

"No, I mean, not that watch. Stella's watch."

Al's eyebrow shot up. "You mean my great-grandmother's watch? Why the hell would you try and steal that? How do you even know her name?" Her hand automatically went to her jacket pocket to make sure it was still safe in there. She felt the shape through the fabric and relaxed.

Her movement didn't escape Hector's attention. Nor did his attention escape Molly's eye. "If you so much as breathe her way wrong, I will smash you."

Al didn't know if Molly had the strength to smash anyone, but she could certainly do some major damage with Big Bertha in her hands.

"I won't. I won't, I just, if I can have the watch, I might be able to slow it down. Or you can. You can crank it yourself and slow things down."

"I can't. It's broken."

"What do you mean, it's broken?" His panic echoed in the car.

"I mean it doesn't work. Never has as long as I've had it."

"But… It should. It shouldn't break down. I made the best watch I could…"

"Wait, what, hold on," Molly said before Al could jump in herself. "You made the watch? How the hell does that work? You're what, thirty, tops? That watch is like a hundred years old!"

Hector looked out the windshield, as if gauging his options. He sighed and leaned back, giving Al a slight smile. "You look like her, you know. Stella Alwilda Taverner. You look so much like her."

Gruff, who'd been silent, opened his eyes.

"Al…" He grabbed her arm and she looked to where he looked, their right. The ground rumbled beneath them.

Al was still deciding what exactly she would do when a transport truck rumbled past her, blowing its horn continuously. It was gone as quickly as it had arrived, swallowed by the mist. As soon as they could no longer see it, they couldn't hear it, either.

"Let's go," Gruff whispered. Al nodded and pressed on the gas.

She was terrified another truck would come barreling out of the mists and take them out. Percival had won his fair share of scrapes, but that was hardly a fair contest.

"Al?" Molly said. "Where are we going? What do we do?"

"You seem to know more about this," Al said to Hector. "Where do we go? Don't talk too much, I need to hear what's going on out there."

"We need somewhere safe where I can fix the watch and get it going again."

"My house," Gruff said. "I should check on the missus. She's probably fine, old spitfire, that one. But still…"

Al nodded and spoke gently. "Of course. But we have to get you to the hospital first, Gruff. It's only two minutes away."

"Al, hospital's gonna be crazy. Let's check on Gretchen first, then we can go. You saw how many accidents there were? And no one in the cars? They've probably all headed to the hospital."

"I wouldn't count on that," Hector whispered from the back.

Al turned on the radio. No stations were coming through, as though the mists were managing to stop even their signals. A thousand questions jumbled in her mind, quarreling with each other on their importance, but one stood out among all others. "I have to find my sister Pete. Are things like this all over?"

Hector looked puzzled. "Your sister's name is Pete?"

"Nickname. Focus. Could she be in danger?"

He looked outside the window. "I think so. I don't see why it

wouldn't be. But I might be able to slow it down. Just for a little bit."

"That doesn't even make sense," Molly mumbled, still clutching Big Bertha. "Am I the only one here who thinks this doesn't make sense?"

Nobody answered. Gruff's old house was ten minutes away. It seemed so far and so long to Al. She wanted her little sister by her side now. She wanted to hold her tight and never let her go. She loosened her grip on the steering wheel. Her hands were starting to cramp up.

"If I give you the watch," Al said, looking back at Hector, who still hesitated to meet her gaze. "You have to promise to give it back. It's mine, and it's all I have left from my family, so you give it back. Understood?"

Hector looked her in the eye this time, his brown eyes sad in the rearview mirror. He nodded.

Before she could reach for the watch, something scratched the side of the car. It sounded like claws.

"Faster, faster, faster…" Gruff started whispering. Alva pressed on the gas just as lilac-blooming branches collapsed on the windshield, cracking it. Screams echoed in the car and outside of it. A man's face followed the branches, twisted by pain as small buds pushed through his skin, erupting in lilac petals. Staring at him, Al's foot loosened from the gas pedal and Percival barely coasted forward.

His mouth formed a perfect "o," as wide as his eyes were. Al couldn't tear her eyes away. From deep within his throat something was pushing its way up, fuzzy insect legs pushing the lips apart as they worked their way out.

"Al, go!" Gruff screamed. Al slammed on the gas and the man went flying. Part of her wanted to stop and make sure he was all right, but a much stronger part of her was terrified and just wanted to keep driving, as quickly and as far as she could.

The front tires jumped up and then the back ones, like they'd hit a speed bump. Hector went flying, hitting his head on the roof of the car.

"Put your seatbelt on, idiot," Molly hissed, reaching around him to fasten it when he just looked at her confused.

"Speed bump. Just a speed bump," Al muttered, her fingers cold on the steering wheel, knowing full well that were no speed bumps here.

"Speed bump," Gruff confirmed, clutching the car door with his good hand.

If they could cross the bridge, they'd be in a more populated area, nearing downtown. There would be help, and people who might know what's happening. They'd check in on Gruff's wife, find shelter, contact Pete and get her.

Find safety.

The mists shifted and cleared, the sun streaming onto the car. Al jumped when it touched her skin, but it didn't burn. The metal

structure of the small bridge jutted around them. They could see clearly to the other side of the bridge, ten metres in length at most.

The front wheels were on the bridge before Hector screamed from behind: "Don't go on the bridge!"

Al slammed on the brakes, but too late – the car was on the bridge.

"Back up slowly," Hector whispered from the back. Al nodded and shifted Percival in reverse, but the car wouldn't budge. The wheels skidded like they were on pure ice.

A shadow to her left made her jump. A man walked by, his coat torn on the side. And another, dragging his feet, wearing only a bathrobe. On the other side of the car, several more walked by, men, women, even children, dragging their feet, their faces slack. Some walked to the middle of the bridge. Others stayed around the car.

Al stopped pressing on the gas and stared at them. No one said a word or breathed. Al glanced at the back seat. Hector was looking intently at the people around them. He leaned forward and she leaned back so he could whisper in her ear. "We'll have one chance. Get ready to move when I tell you to."

She nodded and pointed back and forth, raising her shoulders as though asking a question. He shrugged. It didn't matter which way. She shifted to the first gear, one foot on the clutch and the other on the brake, and waited for his signal.

He looked intently around him. The people continued swaying. The mists bookending the bridge shimmered in the sunlight, translucent wisps dancing toward them. The mists stretched around the car and around each person, not wrapping them fully but keeping some distance, as though inviting them to dance.

Hector narrowed his eyes and looked intently at the wisps nearest them. Al still held her breath, and Gruff and Molly were so silent she could easily forget they were there.

The mists buckled and shapes began to form, gossamer strings turning into large cloaks and hoods, hands stretched out toward the people, who still just swayed there. Translucent hands appeared from misty cloaks and reached for each person. Hector placed his hand on Alva's shoulder. She glanced back and he held up his finger, as though indicating soon.

Her foot left the brakes and trembled over the gas pedal. Percival was stuck anyway and wasn't going anywhere. For now.

She fixed her eyes on the man nearest her, the one wearing a bathrobe and still holding a spilled cup of coffee in his loose hand. Alva steadied her breath, loosened her grip on the steering wheel and waited.

The misty hands reached forward, not for the man's face, but for his chest. The moment stretched into eternity at the hand lingered there, holding the edge of the bathrobe, the translucent cloak shimmering with tiny rainbows of light.

The sun grew brighter, rainbows danced in the air around them, turning beads of water into gems of light. Gossamer hands tightened on clothing.

Columns of water exploded up and Molly screamed. Hector's hand tightened on Al's shoulder and she slammed on the gas, but the wheels were still trapped. The columns collapsed on the bridge, the metal groaning, streams of river breaking apart to avoid each beam and support of the bridge.

The water flashed away and giant dark horses, large teeth bared, trampled the ground around them. The gossamer figures clutched clothing as the horses attacked without pause, their screams echoing against the wall of mist.

They fell on the people, biting them, tearing off limb and head, jets of blood interrupting the perfect prisms and rainbows. The gossamer figures just kept holding the clothing as they became blood soaked, as the silent bodies rolled out of them, to be fully consumed, their blood a river on the bridge.

Molly kept whimpering in the back of the car. Al could barely hear her over the sounds of the horses, their hoofs like thunder.

"It won't go!" Al screamed as she kept pressing on the gas, the car spinning its wheels, burnt rubber almost covering the stench of blood.

"What do we do?" she looked back to Hector, the only one who seemed to have any idea what was going on.

"Don't get out, but can you open the window a crack?" He seemed puzzled as he looked down.

Percival was hardly fancy, with handles to lower the windows. "Can do from my seat," Al said. Her father had loved the two-door feature of the muscle car, but Al didn't always find it the most convenient. And now was definitely one of those less than convenient times.

He nodded. "Get ready."

Al kept her foot on the gas pedal, ignoring the burning smell of her tires skidding uselessly.

Hector reached into his pocket and pulled out what looked like sand. He carefully took some and divvied it up between all of them. Al let go of the gas to take it. Molly looked at Hector with big eyes. "You expect us to go out to put that under the wheels?"

He shook his head quickly. "Just let it drop by your window. It

won't be a perfect circle, but it should be enough to get us off the bridge."

The horses neighed loudly again. They were circling, looking for other victims. So far, they were ignoring Percival and her passengers. The gossamer creatures were more solid now, their cloaks dark and brown as they held the bloody clothing. They headed to the edge of the bridge and seemed to jump or fall off. The horses were slick with blood. They looked around, snorting; their stamping hoofs making the whole bridge shake.

"As soon as we open the window, they'll get our scent." Hector instructed. "They can't get far from the river, so we just have to slam it and go."

"Okay," Al said. She looked at Gruff and Molly. "Molly, can you handle Gruff's window?"

Molly nodded and leaned forward. She still looked terrified, but she was holding it together. Gruff looked grim in determination, and exhausted.

"On three, we lower the windows, and throw down the sand. Close your window as soon as it's done."

All took a deep breath, trying to ignore the blood splattered on her window, or the flank of a large horse as it stomped by.

"Three, two, one..." She lowered her window with two quick cranks of her left hand, threw down the sand and started cranking it back up. The horses screamed and one of them slammed its massive flank against Percival's right side, the car sliding sideways.

Al slammed on the gas, muttering prayers under her breath, and the car took off, the tires skidding just a bit. The horses seemed momentarily startled by the car's quick movement and didn't give chase right away, which was probably what saved them. They slammed into the mists and Al was grateful for its cover. Grateful for the blindness, if it stopped her from having to witness more atrocities like that.

"Al, slow down," Gruff said from beside her. She was well above the speed limit and forced herself to slow down. They were on Main Street now. If help was to be found, it would be here. And more people, hopefully. The chances of smashing into someone or something became very real.

Main Street stretched quietly before them. Al went slowly now, looking for people. She thought she heard the sound of a siren, but it was quickly swallowed by the mists.

"We need to find help," Al said to no one in particular. She was just trying to break the silence before it crushed them all.

"No one can help you now," Hector said. "I have to fix the watch. Buy us time."

"Buy us time from what?" Al said as she looked up. Something dangled over the car from a lamppost. She slowed down a bit as feet hit the windshield and gently slid up, the bare skin sliding on the still slick blood on Percival. Al started her windshield wipers without thinking.

"Time to get ready, I suppose. Or maybe even stop it completely."

Something jumped on her right, smashed against her side window and jumped away. Everyone screamed. The window wasn't broken, and Al accelerated.

"It's going to get worse," Hector mumbled.

"We're not far from my place," Gruff said. "We can get shelter there while we get our bearings."

"What?" Al said, looking to Hector. "What exactly are we trying to stop?"

"What's going on?" Molly whispered. "Those people on the bridge… those horses… that's not even… how does that even happen?"

"It's the veil between the worlds," Hector said, so softly they strained to hear. "The veil between our world and the Old World. It's collapsing. And while we've mostly forgotten about the old folk, they've been studying us and biding their time."

No one spoke. Al had a thousand questions pop into her mind to vanish at once, seeing the grief and fear on Hector's face. Only one question mattered, lit in her mind with the fury of a thousand suns.

She just wanted to know how to be safe. How to keep her own safe.

If even half the fear on Hector's face was justified, she wasn't sure safe was even possible.

Chapter 5

THE STREET was lined with small, similar post-war houses, one-level, slanted roof, vinyl siding. They looked deceptively small. Gruff and Gretchen had managed to raise three children here, and it now seemed too big for just the elderly couple. Or too small.

The mists danced around some houses, as though hugging them. Nothing moved on the street, not even an animal darted across the pavement.

"Looks pretty clear," Al whispered. She pulled into his driveway.

Their backyard was covered in fog.

"Best to stay clear of that," Hector said.

"No shit," Molly replied. Hector looked at her in shock.

"Let's go," Al grabbed Big Bertha and the first aid kit, opened the door and slipped out. Molly helped Gruff and Hector kept a close eye on the mists, which fluttered at the edge of the backyard. They quickly went to the back and found the dilapidated door unlocked.

The door creaked open and they all slipped inside. They closed the door and stood at the back of the kitchen. Black and no-longer-quite-white linoleum tiles covered the floor. The counters were white, as was the small oven. The olive-coloured fridge hummed loudly.

"Gretchen?" Gruff called out. The house would have been deathly quiet if not for the hum of the fridge and the ticking of the grandfather clock in the living room. Gruff waited for an answer, kicked off his work boots and went to remove his coat but grunted and stopped. Al took a step toward him, but he waved her off.

"I'm fine. Really. She's probably asleep. I'll go wake her." He walked slowly down the hallway. Gruff was pushing seventy. It had never really struck Al before how that made him old. Right now, watching his slow, careful walk, it was all she could think of.

"This house is time trapped in the 70s," Molly whispered in awe. "They've even got the rusty old can opener to prove it!"

Molly walked into the kitchen, opening drawers and giggling at the old utensils she found. Al shook her head and focused on Hector instead.

"All right, make this fast," Al reached into her coat and felt the smooth cover of the watch. She handed it to him. His eyes filled with tears as he looked at the watch. He ran his fingers over it, as though feeling each tiny engraved line. As though the pine tree and the tiny house had been his, once. His hands shook slightly as he popped it open. The glass face was intact, the tiny gold and blue inlays of the timepiece glinting in the dull fluorescent light. The arrows pointed at 10:24. Always 10:24.

He stared at the time, running his fingers over the glass slowly.

"Family legend has it that's the time she passed away. That the watch just stopped then, and wouldn't restart," Al said, not too sure why. Maybe to snap him out of it. His grief was almost palpable from where she stood. It was unnerving her as much as the fog.

She looked more closely at him. His coat was greenish brown, all wool. His hair was short but still longer than he seemed used to, flicking it back even though it barely reached his eyes.

"I have to get this moving again," he whispered, to the watch or to her, Al wasn't sure.

Al nodded nevertheless. "And that'll... I can't believe I'm saying this, but that'll stop the mists?"

"I hope," he gave her a weak grin.

"Al," Molly said as she walked up beside her, breaking her out of her reverie. "I still can't get a cell signal. Or a radio signal," she pointed to an old transistor radio on the counter.

"The mists will block all of that," Hector said. He looked up at them, apologetic. "I need to concentrate. Please."

He spread out a leather case and unfurled it to reveal tiny silver tools. He set magnifying lenses on his nose. Al stared at him as he diverted all his attention to the watch. His clothing didn't look old, but the style was old. And the spectacles were definitely not today's standard. And, the tools, the ability to repair watches, his knowledge of her great-grandmother's watch and name…

A shiver ran down her back. Hector leaned in close to the watch. The back was popped off, and he gently but expertly moved tiny gears around.

Al needed to clear her head.

Molly sat cross-legged on the couch and kept trying to get her smartphone to connect to something, looking intently at it.

The morning's events still seemed like a dream. She expected to wake up any moment now and make a joke with Pete about the dream. Pete would love it, with her love of old stories and folklore.

Her heart skipped a beat. Pete was smart. She could take care of herself. She hoped that the bus had been late. Otherwise they would be nearing Lindsay now. Or maybe, like Hector suspected, this was everywhere and not just here and it didn't matter where Pete was.

She shook her head, annoyed at herself. Pete was smart. Pete could take care of herself. She had made that clear to Alva on several occasions, in fact. Picturing her sister's red, angry face made her smile. She was fine. Whatever this was, it was probably localized anyway. Some weird gas leak making them all hallucinate.

She forced the sight of the horses tearing apart the people on the bridge out of her mind and headed to the washroom. She splashed cold water on her face and felt better for it.

For a second, she thought she saw something flicker behind her in the mirror. She turned around, but nothing was there. She took a deep breath and exited the bathroom. Mists lined the floor. Alva took a deep breath and called out.

"Gruff?"

She took two steps to the master bedroom and peeked in, her breath collapsing back into her lungs and her hand going to her mouth.

In the middle of the room, over the large king size bed covered in bedding as dark as the wood posts of the old bed, Gretchen floated, her long nightgown turning slowly like a great ball gown, her arms gently held up by a young man. He was made of light, the mists feeding his appearance as he shifted in and out, wearing at times armour of a knight of old, at other times a fine tuxedo and top hat. He held Gretchen gently, twirling with her in the air, staring into her eyes as she stared back. Stray ringlets of gray hair escaped her nightcap, but she looked younger than her sixty-some years.

She smiled and her hand went up to man's cheek, gently stroking it as her right foot lifted back a bit. Perfectly slow dance steps were performed on the ballroom floor of glittering mist.

Gruff stood not far from the door, his cheeks glinting with fresh tears and starry mists. He looked at her with such tenderness that it broke Al's heart.

The dancers shifted a bit and Al could see that her feet and hands were slowly turning to mist, joining the man in whatever state he existed.

Gretchen looked at her hand, seemingly surprised for a few moments before placing it back on the shoulder of her companion. She leaned into him, closing her eyes and smiling as they held each other, her features, dress and nightcap all turning to light. The mists dissipated around them, the light shifting to rainbow and then vanishing completely.

Al could still see the light of the dancers as she blinked, in the dark curtained room.

"She's finally found her knight in shining armour," Gruff whispered, still looking at the spot where his wife had just vanished, blinking away the tears and streaks of light.

"Gruff…" Al didn't know what to say.

"It's okay, Al," he said softly. "I just… need a moment."

The mists had retreated, and the room seemed deathly quiet now. Al nodded and stepped out into the corridor. An old picture smiled at her from the wall, Gretchen and Gruff, young and full of hope on their wedding day. Her blond hair curled under her pulled back veil, his top hat slightly crooked on his head.

He'd been her knight in shining armour, once.

Al grabbed the picture, not sure why. She didn't want Gruff to see it when he came out of the room. She didn't want him to lose himself further in memories of what might have been.

She didn't want to lose him to the mists, or the past.

Chapter 6

THE COGS were tiny, and Hector's hands felt numb as he touched them.

He remembered feeling every edge when he'd first built the watch, what was both a year ago and lifetimes ago. Now, he couldn't feel the tiny pieces of metal save for the pressure on his numb fingertips. Calluses that would take several more lifetimes to heal blocked the sensations of a life that was so far gone it might as well have been a dream.

He focused on the tiny gears. The silence was oppressive. The mists might infiltrate at any moment, or pierce the house, and the enemy would swarm.

He forced his breathing to relax and his hands to stop shaking. The quiet before the storm. It had been such a clichéd saying. Until he'd been on the fields of France, in a rat-ridden stinking hole, waiting for the bullets to start flying again. Hoping they would, so he wouldn't have to wait anymore.

The watch had suffered from age. Age and neglect. Oh, they'd taken care of her casing. It had been polished, and even the original glass was still intact. But it was the inside that mattered.

Stella had known that. But Stella wouldn't have known what to do with it, save to keep it. Stella's great-granddaughter, Alva, walked into the room, clutching a portrait, as white as ash. He resisted the urge to stop working on the watch and go to her. She didn't know him. Stella hadn't mentioned him, ever, as far as he could tell.

Maybe it made things easier. Maybe it was for the best.

He hesitated and resumed his work on the watch. She sat on a stool at the kitchen island and stared at the watch.

He sighed. He couldn't ignore her, no matter how much he wanted to. She looked like Stella, or parts of her did. The way she shifted her feet now. The intelligence behind the hazel eyes, as though always thinking, always planning. The flush of her cheek. The rust colour of her hair. He looked at her and saw parts of Stella, and it hurt him more than he could afford to acknowledge.

But, like a watch, it was the inside that counted. And, growing up in a world so different than Stella's, he had no doubt she would be vastly different.

"Are you all right?" he asked softly. She looked up, surprised at first. Then she shrugged.

"You said you can stop it?" she whispered.

He hesitated and nodded. "If I can get this watch going again,

then yes, I can."

Alva nodded. She resumed looking at the watch, and so did he.

Molly joined them. "Are we just going to keep moving like none of this is weird?"

Alva gave her friend a smile. The care in it formed a lump in Hector's throat. A smile so much like Stella's.

"It's weird, Molly. I just…" She paused. Gruff walked into the room and sat down on a stool. The old man looked even more tired.

"Let's look at your arm," Molly whispered. He didn't argue or struggle, just letting Alva and Molly work on him. Hector had seen this before, on the field. The breaking.

He slipped the last gear in place and closed the back of the watch gently. He ran his fingers along the inscription, hidden within the watch, wishing his fingers could feel every groove.

"You're done?" Alva asked.

He nodded. "I'm going to wind the watch. This should stop the mists."

They all looked at him expectantly. He held his breath as he wound it carefully, the hands of the watch moving in jerky movements, but moving nonetheless. Away from when Stella had stopped the watch.

We'll see each other again, my love. Just keep your head down and your heart open, and we'll see each other again.

The watch went to two o'clock, ticked forward once. Then it began ticking backward.

Hector looked at it, puzzled. The mechanism wasn't set to be a timer clock, yet…

Time isn't the matter. Time will always be on our side, for our love exists outside of it. It's the world that might be the challenge, my love. It's how we react to its challenges that will keep us together, or break us apart.

The watch was counting down. Three hours. Three measly hours was all he had managed to win back.

The house hummed as electricity returned to it. A radio turned on in the living room. Molly looked down at her small device. He'd love to open it and see what made it work.

"Everything's back up! I'll text Pete," Molly exclaimed.

"Thank you," Alva mumbled, then she turned to Hector. "Is it over?" Hector closed the front of the watch and looked to them, his eyes coming to a rest on Alva. He couldn't save Stella, anymore.

He shook his head. "For now. We have to get going and find your sister. I don't know how long it'll hold."

Molly looked up to him, as did Alva. Their eyes were wide and terrified. Gruff just looked down at the counter. Broken.

"But I think I can find a safe spot for us," he added. Molly looked down right away, but Alva held his eyes, as though measuring the kind of man he was. He found himself straightening his back and looking back, unflinching.

"She's okay!" Molly shrieked. "Their bus went off the road and they're trapped in it, but we can get them out!" Alva and Molly spoke quickly back and forth on details of where she was, how they'd get there, what supplies they needed, but Hector ignored them, running his fingers on the watch, lovingly etched details he could no longer feel.

He couldn't save Stella, but maybe he could find a way to save her children. If only he could move quickly enough.

Chapter 7

THE MISTS had lifted and left disaster in their wake. Entire houses had collapsed. Blood lined the streets like snow in winter, and bodies were abandoned like trash on the sides of roads. People were coming out of their houses like they'd woken up from a bad dream. The wounded were being tended to by paramedics when possible, otherwise by passers-by or loved ones.

Alva clutched the steering wheel and proceeded carefully down the residential roads, avoiding any main arteries. There were lots of accidents, but not as many as might have happened had it been later in the day, when more people were on their way to work. Small blessings.

She turned Percival on someone's lawn to avoid a gap that had materialized in the road, like something had crunched it down. Molly lowered the passenger side window and apologized to the owner, who sat on his steps without moving. He barely acknowledged her.

"Should we stop?" Molly asked, rolling her window back up.

"We need to get your sister," Hector said right away. "We might not have much time,"

Alva nodded, but glanced back at the homeowner. She thought of Steve and Louise in the shop, and how she'd left them behind. And Jack, who she'd run away from. If her entire life was to be judged on how she did in that shop, she would fail miserably. She hadn't found the courage to help them, but she certainly could find it to save her sister.

"Pete says the bus still won't open its doors. A few of the students were hurt, but not bad."

"Okay. We get Pete and help those kids off the bus. Then we get out of here and go..." She looked back to Hector.

"North," he offered.

"North." She repeated to reaffirm.

Gruff sat silently in the back and gazed out the window. Al wanted to take his hand and tell him everything would be okay, but they still couldn't reach his children, or his grandchildren. And he'd just witnessed his wife vanish, or die, or whatever that was.

She wasn't sure she could tell him everything would be okay. The lie refused to tumble from her lips.

The yellow bus had come to a stop in a field by a quiet road in the country. Al pulled Percival to the side of the road and threw on her four ways, for good measure. There were no emergency vehicles or any other vehicles around. The yellow bus was perfectly quiet and stopped by a shimmering lake. Al felt nauseated at the thought that the creatures from the bridge might have gotten her sister, too.

She exited the vehicle with Hector and Molly. She grabbed Big Bertha and her tool belt. They needed to get those doors open somehow.

The sun was comforting. There was no breeze blowing, and it was turning into a warm day for fall. The field was still covered in green grass, running down a small hill toward the bus, reeds the only thing separating it from the water.

"If anything happens, we meet back at Percival, okay?" Al instructed. Molly nodded and looked at Percival as though noting its position in the deepest trenches of her memory.

"Let's go," Al said, walking toward the bus. Molly waved, and Al grinned when she spotted Pete through the window. The bus's windows were all closed and it was covered in vines.

"No wonder they couldn't get out," Molly muttered. "Hope you have garden shears in your tool belt."

"Wire cutters. That oughta do." She pulled them out and grinned.

"You would have made an awesome scout," Molly said.

They reached the bus and dozens of faces looked at them through the windows. Al focused on Pete. A rare smile of gratitude spread

her lips apart. Her face seemed even paler than usual under her veil of long dyed black hair. Al smiled back and headed around the bus, near the water, to cut the vines keeping the doors closed. They were thick and it took all of her strength to get through them. She just needed to get the doors free and they could all leave.

Maybe she could get all of the vines off and they could get the bus going again. Pete would ride with them, but the bus could head back into town. It seemed sensible enough.

Al had just managed to cut one vine when Molly came around to join her.

"This will take a while," Al said, grunting.

"Al…" Molly whispered, pointing to the river.

Al's blood turned cold and she turned around slowly. The waters were still calm, but the shimmer on it moved in patterns. They had formed curved lines and danced up and down, toward the shore

then away again. She was cold and realized the sun wasn't touching her anymore, despite the fact that it still shimmered on the water and there wasn't a cloud in the sky.

She stood in a shadow. The bus was casting a shadow on her, even though the sun was in full sight. And on this side of the bus. Molly grabbed her arm and pulled her away from the door. Al was too stunned to fight back.

They reached the sun again, but the shadows of a tree inched towards them. The shadow from the bus began shifting as well. Towards them.

As though it hunted them.

Chapter 8

HECTOR SAW the shadows shift and he clicked on the button atop the watch to pop the front open. The hands of the watch were quivering with effort to continue forward, skipped and jumped irregularly, twitching as they reached 10:24. The time of Stella's death.

He tried winding it again, but the whole mechanism refused to shift, as though the gears had gained a mind of their own.

He closed it, pocketed the watch as he started running toward Alva and Molly.

They were in a field, beside water, in tall grass… He could see the sun dancing on the waters, could smell the mists on the air, a sickening mix of lavender and sugar.

"We have to go!" he screamed, trying to pull Alva away from the strange shadows. Screams rose from within the bus, echoing in the still air around them.

"Not without Pete!" Alva screamed, pulling out of his grasp and running to a window that was still out of the shadows, her sister looking at her through it, the only one not screaming in the bus.

The only one who still had hope.

Al cut at the vines and pulled at them with her bare hands. Thorns began to grow on them and she ignored the cuts, cursing her own blood for making them slick. Molly joined her in pulling, her best friend's mouth drawn in quiet determination.

Pete was banging the window now, trying to force it open from inside.

"Move aside," Hector said, pulling sand from his pocket and throwing it on the vines. The vines browned and shriveled a bit, but it still took all three of them to pull them loose.

"Pete, open the window," Al screamed over the terrified screams from within the bus. Blood splattered one of the back windows and Al forced herself to focus on Pete. Keep looking at me, she willed her sister.

"Just open the window!" She screamed, wishing the despair didn't ring in her voice so deeply.

Pete was banging on it, but it wouldn't go down, wouldn't budge or open.

"Stand back!" Al screamed, and she slammed Big Bertha again the window. It cracked on the first hit, and shattered on the second.

"Come on," Molly was pulling Pete out of the window before Al had regained her footing from the second hit.

"What about the others?" Pete screamed.

The day turned dark and winds slammed into them. Al looked up. The sun was still out, but it was dark. The shadows that would usually be cast on a sunny day suddenly turned to light. Hector grabbed them and pulled them out of the bus's shadow of light, moments before it lit everything on fire.

The scream rose to a fervent pitch for one second in the bus before stopping, the scent of burnt flesh tossed about in the wind. The water surged behind them and columns of it danced up, taking equine and human shapes.

"Run, run, run!" Molly screamed, grabbing Pete and Alva's arms. Hector led the way. Mists came off the water and slammed into them, knocking them to their knees.

Percival wasn't far, now. Just a few more metres. They could get in and drive away. Gruff was screaming at them to hurry. He was in the passenger's seat, the car on and ready to move, the driver door open and the seat leaned forward, beckoning its passengers.

The mists danced back and forth and they pulled themselves up.

"Look out!" Hector screamed at Al, his face contorted with grief as she looked down. She'd stepped into a perfect circle of mushrooms. She felt something zap up her leg, but before she could scream or even fear what was happening to her, Molly tackled her from behind. She was either moving her, or she hadn't seen what had been happening, too frantic to escape.

Al fell down. Hector and Pete helped her up. Al turned to grab Molly and keep running, but her hand was stiff as she took it.

Al met her best friend's eyes. Where there was usually laughter and kindness was only fear. The hand she held was a branch now. Al pulled her hand out as thorns pierced her skin.

"Alva?" Molly managed to say in a broken voice, the tears streaking down skin turning to bark as her face vanished completely, swallowed by bark, leaf and thorn.

Al stared. She was gone in an instant, in mist and the strange dark day, swallowed by a still forming bush, branches writhing up and reaching for them, like hands pleading for help.

"Molly?" She repeated, reaching forward. Hector pulled her back. Alva looked at him in anger, but stopped herself from snapping when she saw the tears lining Pete's face. She placed an arm around Pete's shoulders as yellow blooms erupted on the rose bush that had once been Al's best friend.

Not yellow like the sun. Yellow like Molly's hair had been. The only rosebush that would ever bear that colour. The only one that ever should.

"We have to go," Hector whispered. The winds began howling. Al's braid whipped sideways, but the rosebush wasn't fazed at all. Like it didn't belong to this world anymore.

To any world.

"I'll come back. I promise," she whispered into the gale, helped

Pete and Hector into the back and shut Percival's door to the howling winds.

Al clutched the steering wheel, watched the yellow roses vanish in a sea of mists, and pulled the car off the road, away from her friend, toward more mist, to face a world she no longer understood.

The rosebush continued to bloom behind them, each flower covered in a fine layer of freshly-cried dew.

Epilogue

THE WATCH lay quietly in Hector's hand. No matter what he did, he couldn't get it to wind up. He couldn't even open it.

Stella's other great-granddaughter sat sullenly beside him. He missed Molly, and he'd only known her for a short time. He understood what the Taverner girls were going through. What it felt like to lose your world.

To lose everything.

He understood the grief. The anger. The madness.

He held the watch in his hand and looked outside. The spare sand he'd brought was almost gone. He'd used so much of it already, just trying to keep them safe.

And if he used too much, he wouldn't be around to help them anymore.

He looked up to see Al, back in the driver's seat, observing him from the rearview mirror. Her eyes were still grief-lined, but determined. She intended to see her sister safe, if that was even possible.

The question was in her eyes now. Would they live?

He held her gaze for a time before looking away.

He had no answer to give her.

- The End of Nigh 1 -

The Tale Continues

Nigh 2

Other books by Marie Bilodeau

Heirs of a Broken Land
Princess of Light
Warrior of Darkness
Sorceress of Shadows

Destiny
Destiny's Blood
Destiny's Fall
Destiny's War

www.mariebilodeau.com

www.ingramcontent.com/pod-product-compliance
Lightning Source LLC
Chambersburg PA
CBHW030532310726
48979CB00010B/1890/J

* 9 7 8 0 9 9 4 0 4 3 9 1 7 *